"Let it Go Little Monkey!"

Pamela Alejandra

"Let it Go Little Monkey!"

Written & Illustrated

By

Pamela Alejandra

Dedication

To The Valpiga's new generation...

Paulo Antonio & Maximo Ignacio:

Thank you for being here!

Thank you for all the Love you inspire

You are already perfect;
So feel free to explore the fullest of this human experience.

Never fear mistakes; but fiercely learn from them.

Overcome all circumstances to the greatest imaginable scenario
In all Nobility; Gracefully and passionately at the same time;

While making warm memories and friends along the way.

Walk with pride of where you have come from;
it does not determine where you will go

May your raising be a joyous one!
Remember to have fun!

See you soon!
See you Chiempre!

Los Ama,
La Tia Pame
(Pah-Meh)

In this story of a monkey; a peanut; a box and a hole...

Sunny morning in the deep jungle.

Tall grasses and swirling vines
        shimmer with the sunrays shining through the leaves.

                            All beings are happy and free;

            Enjoying their morning routines;
        as they realize morning routines work best for them!

Diligently disciplined ants
            grab all necessary supplies for the colony.

Hunters busy with their agenda

cleaning weapons and prepping traps;

Anticipating a good hunt.

Slight breeze cooles the air,

as the birds sang morning chirps

and the monkeys played in the trees.

Hunters try all their best methods and techniques
                                    to catch these monkeys;

Only the monkeys appear substantially smarter than the hunters,

          and get all the trapped fruit from the nets anyways!

The jungle is a very fertile territory;

Monkeys have everything they can imagine
                              and a great quality of life!

                    Assortment of fresh fruits;
                         vines to swing from;
                                    family;
                                    friends
even music provided by the birds in the trees!

An attentive audience is out watching

                    and the hunters use that to their advantage!

They know of the monkeys' natural tendency for curiosity
                                        and exploration,

Since there is nothing in nature that is square or cubical;

This wooden box is a great new thing to explore!

For some reason humans have an interesting relationship to square objects:

They live in square houses;
Go inside their square garages;
To get into their square looking car;
Drive onto a rectangular highway;
Unto another square garage;
And then the elevator…
To get to their square cubical they work from;
And stare at square devices all day;
They eat cereal from boxes;
And clean with sponges!

Watch out for those squares!

Hunters create a box trap,

with a hole on top big enough for the monkeys to fit their hand in;

but not to take their fist out!

They place roasted peanuts inside the box
                              to attract the monkey's senses;

And they are well pleased with the results.

Some monkeys don't want to let go of the peanut
when they sense danger near

in the desperation of attachment...

and trying to escape, they get in the nets and get caught!

In the light of recent events;
                    and seeing many of their friends missing;

the little monkeys gather to seek council from an older monkey;

You see;

If they had learned to let go of that peanut soon enough;

      They would not have gotten caught in the nets

         and would have had enough time to run away free.

Only those who did not want to let go of those peanuts
                                    got caught…

In this monkeys life; there is a peanut.

In your human life..

Do you have something in your life like a "peanut"
                                        you can identify with?

Something that doesn't allow you to be...

                        the best version of YourSelf.

                    Like a self inflicted limitation;
                                        Attachments
                            Disbelieves in ourselves
    The adoption of someone else's limiting story as your own?
                                            hmm?

Feel free to upgrade your current life existence;

Take a little time for yourself…

Bring about any current thought that doesn't serve your life.

Imagine this gone; Imagine it well gone!

Upgrade your imagination a few notches if you need to…

Imagine it well enough,

To the point of sensing the experience of the biochemistry of
your brain and body change withouth that thought...
                              Or the way you are currently seeing it.

Think about that life situation exclusively in a way that it
serves You…

How and what do you think about this now?

In that state of being... ...take a few breaths;

in gratitude for the expansion of life experience;
see how life unfolds to the consistency of your own life rhythm.

Take as much time to yourself as you feel inspired to do so.

You are worth absolutely all of the time you invest in yourself.

Thank you for Loving YourSelf so much!

Just Be.

HEALING TO **THRIVE** LOVE ART TOUR

HEALING TO THRIVE LOVE ART TOUR

Thank you!

CPSIA information can be obtained
at www.ICGtesting.com
Printed in the USA
BVHW022220080921
616423BV00007B/118